# The Three Billy Goats Gruff

This edition published 1995 by
Greenwich Editions
Unit 7, 202–208 New North Road
London N1 7BJ

Printed in Singapore

ISBN 0-8628-8002-5

Adapted by Elizabeth Hastings from a Norwegian folk tale
collected by Asbjørnsen and Moe and translated by Sir George
Dasent (1858). Text © 1992 Random House Ltd. Illustrations
© 1992 Robert Chapman. All rights reserved. Random House Ltd,
20 Vauxhall Bridge Road, London SW1V 2SA.

# The Three Billy Goats Gruff

Retold by Elizabeth Hastings
Illustrated by Robert Chapman

Greenwich Editions

Once upon a time there were three billy-goats, a small billy-goat, a middle-sized billy-goat and a big billy-goat, and each was called Gruff.

The three billy-goats Gruff could see a meadow in the distance where the grass was green and good to eat, and off they set to go to it. But they found a wide river in the way with only one bridge across, and below that bridge was a huge and horrible troll with great round eyes and a nose as long as a poker.

The small billy-goat Gruff began to cross the bridge – TRIP TRAP.

"Who's that crossing my bridge?" roared the troll.

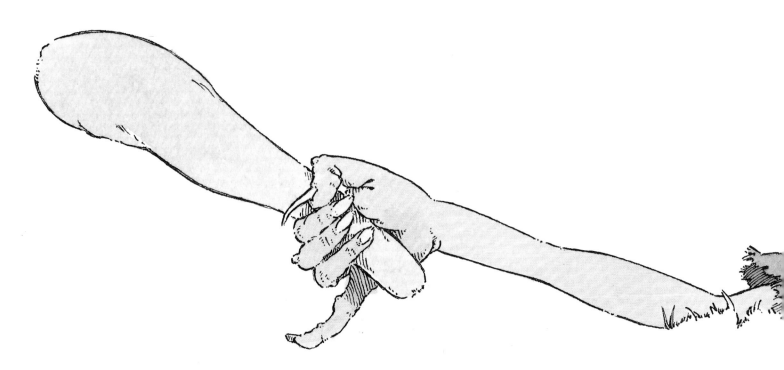

"It's only me, the small billy-goat Gruff, and I'm going to the meadow to eat grass," said the small billy-goat in a small voice.

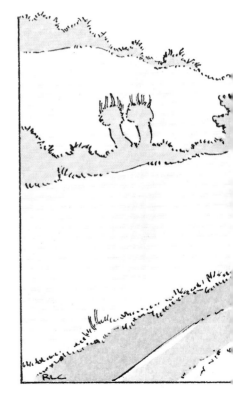

"I shall gobble you up!" roared the troll.

"Oh, don't do that. Wait till my brother comes along. He's much bigger and fatter than I am."

"Be off with you then," said the troll.

Soon after, the middle-sized billy-goat Gruff began to cross the bridge – TRIP TRAP TRIP.

TRIP TRAP TRIP

"Who's that crossing my bridge?" roared the troll.

"It's only me, the middle-sized billy-goat Gruff,
and I'm going to the meadow to eat grass,"
said the middle-sized billy-goat in a
middle-sized voice.

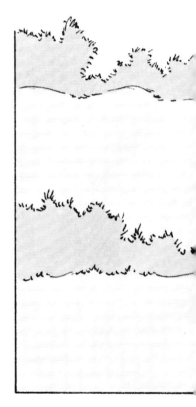

"I shall gobble you up!" roared the troll.

"Oh, don't do that. Wait till my brother comes along. He's much bigger and fatter than I am."

"Be off with you then," said the troll.

At long last the big billy-goat began to cross the bridge — TRIP TRAP TRIP TRAP.

"Who's that crossing my bridge?" roared the troll.

"It's me, BIG BILLY-GOAT GRUFF," shouted the big billy-goat in a very big voice.

"I'm coming to gobble you up!" roared the troll.

"OH NO, YOU'RE NOT!" shouted the big billy-goat Gruff. He charged at the troll, tossed him in the air with his huge horns and threw him SPLASH into the river. Then the big billy-goat Gruff crossed the bridge to join the middle-sized billy-goat Gruff and the small billy-goat Gruff on the other side, and they all went off together to the green meadow where they ate to their hearts' content.